KU-533-010

Ben & Holly's Little Kingdom™

The Little Forest

Elf Oak Wood

Gaston's Cave

Elf Windmill

Little Castle

The Meadow

Great Elf Tree

Elf Farm

Mrs Witch's House

Royal Golf Course

N
W E
S

The Bramble Woods

Frog Pond

The Pine Forest

The Lost Egg

Today's adventure starts in the Little Forest . . . .

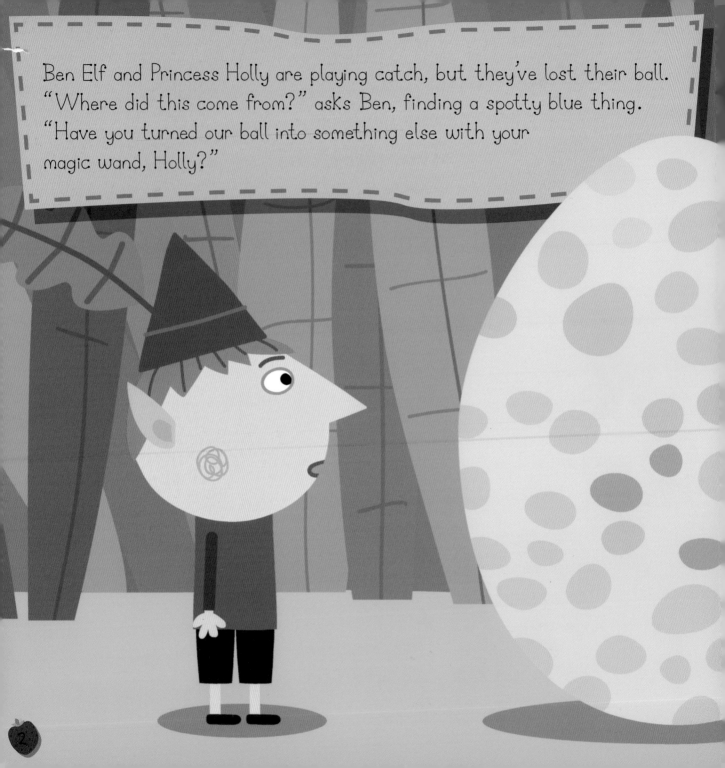

Ben Elf and Princess Holly are playing catch, but they've lost their ball. "Where did this come from?" asks Ben, finding a spotty blue thing. "Have you turned our ball into something else with your magic wand, Holly?"

"No, Ben. I think it's some sort of egg,"
cries Holly. "Let's see what Nanny thinks."

3

"That's a bird's egg," explains Nanny Plum.
"Good day!" shouts the Wise Old Elf. "I think you'll find this is a blackbird's egg and there's a baby chick inside."
"Oooh!" gasp Ben and Holly, excitedly.

"How do you know there's a chick inside?" asks Ben.
"You can hear tapping," explains the Wise Old Elf. "Listen."
Tap! Tap! Tap!

6

"Oooh!" smiles Holly. "Can we look after it, Nanny?" "No, Holly," replies Nanny Plum. "You must never collect the eggs of wild birds. We must find its mummy instead."

Nanny Plum decides they should build a nest to keep the egg warm, while they find the mummy bird. Just then, King Thistle arrives.

"Your Majesty!" says Nanny. "If you could sit on the egg to keep it warm, while we build a nest, that would be kind."
"Very well," replies the King, sitting right on top of the egg.

"I say," states King Thistle.
"This is jolly uncomfortable!"
"We'll be as quick as we can,"
says the Wise Old Elf.

The elves pick up sticks and the fairies find thistledown for the nest. Then Nanny Plum says the magic words and **ZAP!** A perfect nest appears.

11

King Thistle jumps off the egg. **CRACK!**
"Oh, Daddy!" gasps Holly. "You've broken the egg!"
"No he hasn't," smiles Ben Elf. "The egg is hatching, look!" Suddenly, a little chick peers out of the broken eggshell. Cheep! Cheep!

"The chick is following Nanny!" cries Holly. "Don't follow me," says Nanny. "I'm not your mummy."

"The chick is hungry," says the Wise Old Elf. "It wants worms and other insects."

"Er . . . Gaston is an insect," begins Ben. Oh dear, now Gaston looks very nervous! "Gaston, maybe you should stand back a bit!" suggests Princess Holly.

"We can try worm charming to feed the chick," says the Wise Old Elf, stamping his feet on the ground. Thud! Thud! "The worms will think it is raining, so they will come up to breathe."

Everyone stamps their feet on the ground really hard. **THUD! THUD! THUD!**
But the worms are just too quick to catch.

"The baby bird is very hungry now," cries Holly. "The mummy bird normally comes when her baby calls out to her," says the Wise Old Elf. "But the baby bird is not chirping loud enough."

18

KABOOM! Oh dear, Nanny Plum has made the chick bigger, so its chirp will be louder, but she didn't mean to make the chick enormous!

"CHEEP! CHEEP!" chirps the baby bird, very loudly.

"How long will the spell last?" asks King Thistle.

"Er . . . it could last a minute, or a week!" replies Nanny Plum, nervously.

Hooray! The spell has worn off and the mummy bird has arrived. She must have heard the loud chirping! The chick is very happy and flies off with its mummy.

"Nanny. Now I'm hungry!" says Holly, her tummy rumbling.
"How about some nice juicy worms?" smiles Ben.
"Yuck!" everyone cries. "Hee, hee, hee!"

23